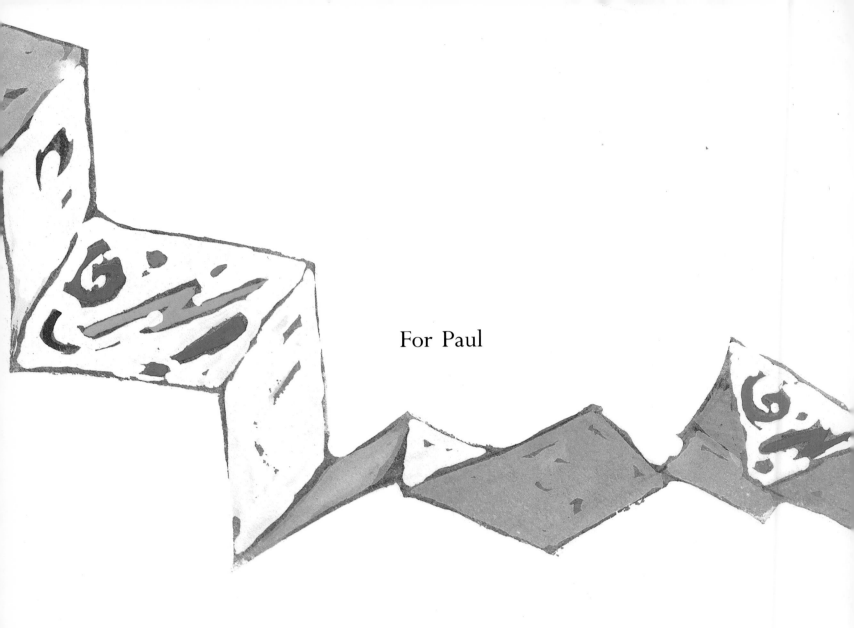

For Paul

Copyright © 1991 by Simon Henwood

All rights reserved

First published in Great Britain by ABC, All Books for Children,
a division of The All Children's Company, Ltd, 1991

First American edition, 1991

Library of Congress catalog card number: 90-28883

Published simultaneously in Canada by HarperCollins*CanadaLtd*

Printed in Hong Kong

the Troubled Village

Simon Henwood

Farrar, Straus and Giroux

New York

Once there was a village where the people competed with each other for trouble.

"I have more problems than you do."

"No, you don't. If only you knew how hard life is for me."

The longer the list of problems they had, the prouder everyone seemed to become.

By fixing his neighbour's roof in the middle of the night, Mr Jones made sure that the Smith family had one less problem to add to its list.

One night, there was a terrible storm.

All the people were busy adding to their
troubles by pulling off roof tiles and breaking
windows, trying to make it look as though the
storm had caused all the damage. Suddenly,
the most terrible thing imaginable happened; the
sort of awful trouble that every villager dreamed
of having.

The sky fell in.

Not all of it, of course, but a hole about as big as a duck pond.

Everyone gathered around where it had fallen. No one had seen the sky so close before.

One little boy tried to touch a star, and slipped and fell in.

The villagers panicked and, trying to save the little boy, ended up falling in after him.

The last villager only just managed to get a
good, firm grasp, and pulled them all to safety.

Now they had to put the sky back up.

Everyone agreed it was too great a problem for one person, so, for the very first time, they all worked together.

Getting the sky up wasn't too difficult, because it was no heavier than a carpet, but making it stay up was.

No glue or sticky tape would hold it in place.

There was only one thing to do — a large pole had to be brought to use as a giant prop.

The pole was brought and positioned. As one tip of the pole reached the stars, the villagers looked at the other end in dismay.

The pole was two feet short.

From that moment on,
each villager took it in turns
to hold the pole that propped
up the sky, and any other
troubles were soon forgotten.